For Cheryl

First Edition

Reinforced binding

20 19 18 17 16 15 14 13

F850-6835-5-12362

Printed in Singapore

Library of Congress Cataloging-in-Publication Data on file.

ISBN: 0-7868-1869-7

Visit www.hyperionbooksforchildren.com and www.mowillems.com

The Pigeon Finds a Hot Dog!

words and pictures by mo willems

HYPERION BOOKS FOR CHILDREN/New York

An Imprint of Disney Book Group

I have a
question.

I've never
had a
hot dog
before....

What do they
taste like?

Woodson

Of course!
Enjoy!

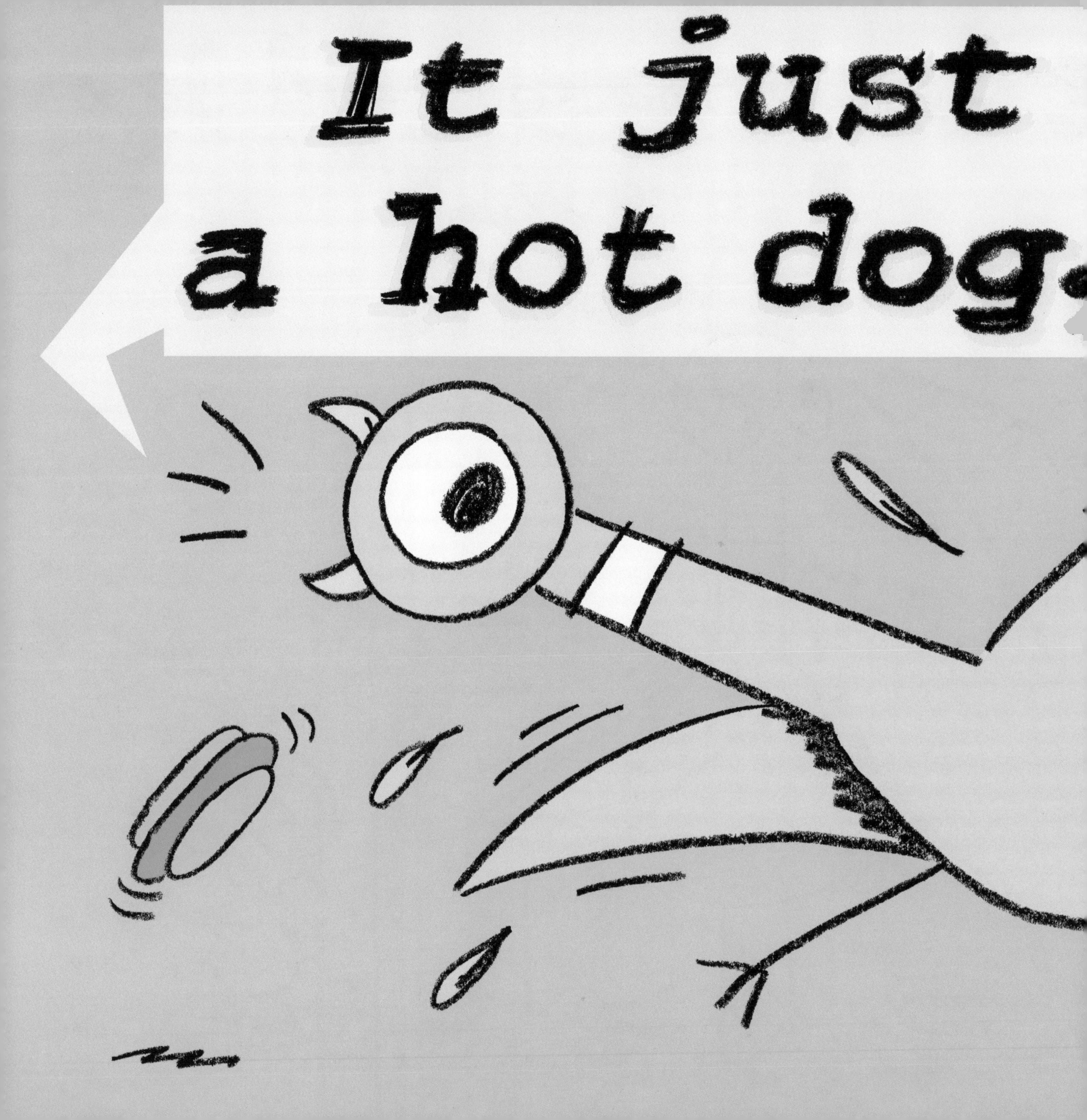
It just
a hot dog.

tastes like okay!?

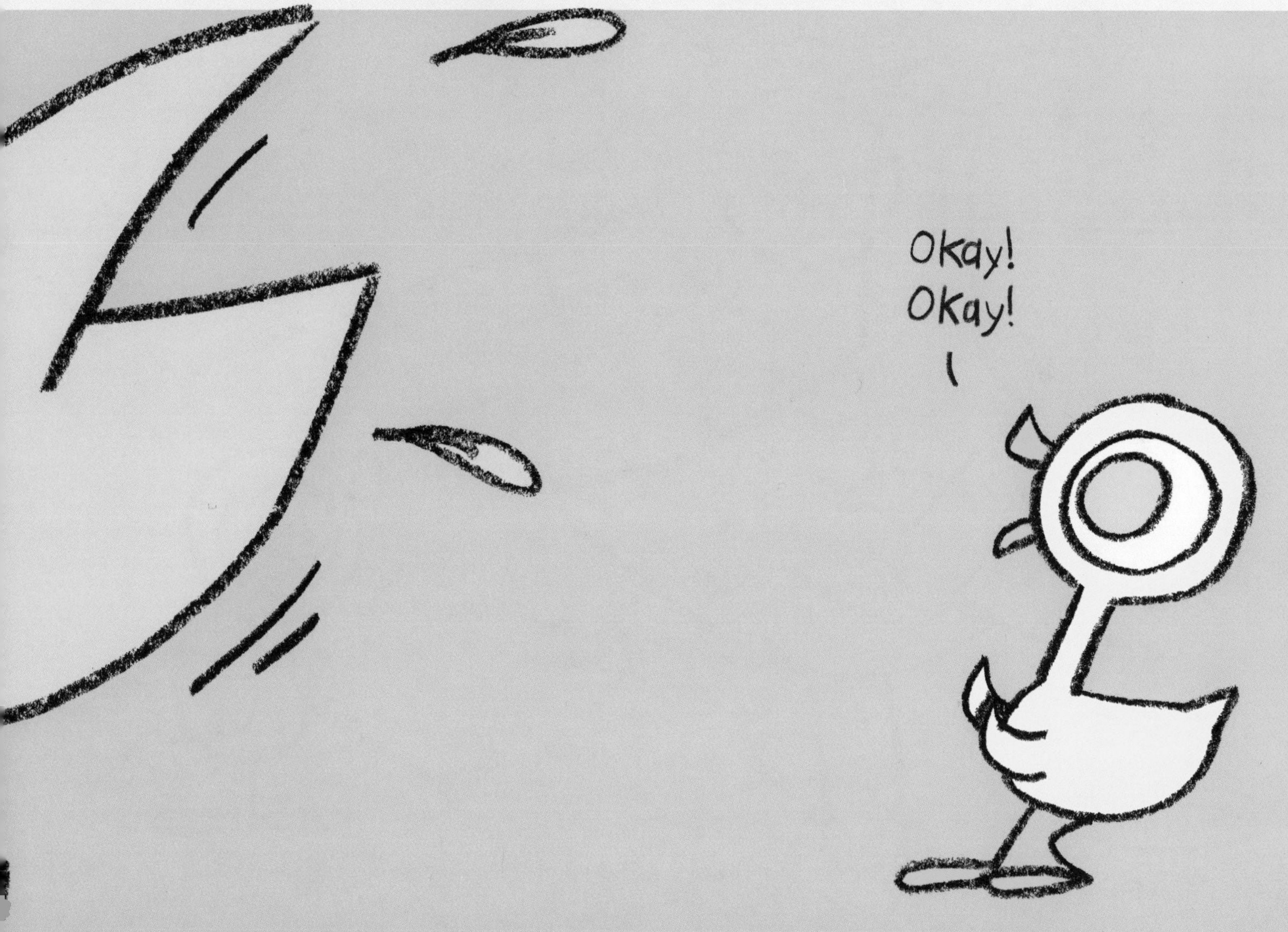

I think
I've got
an idea.

You know, you're pretty smart for a duckling.

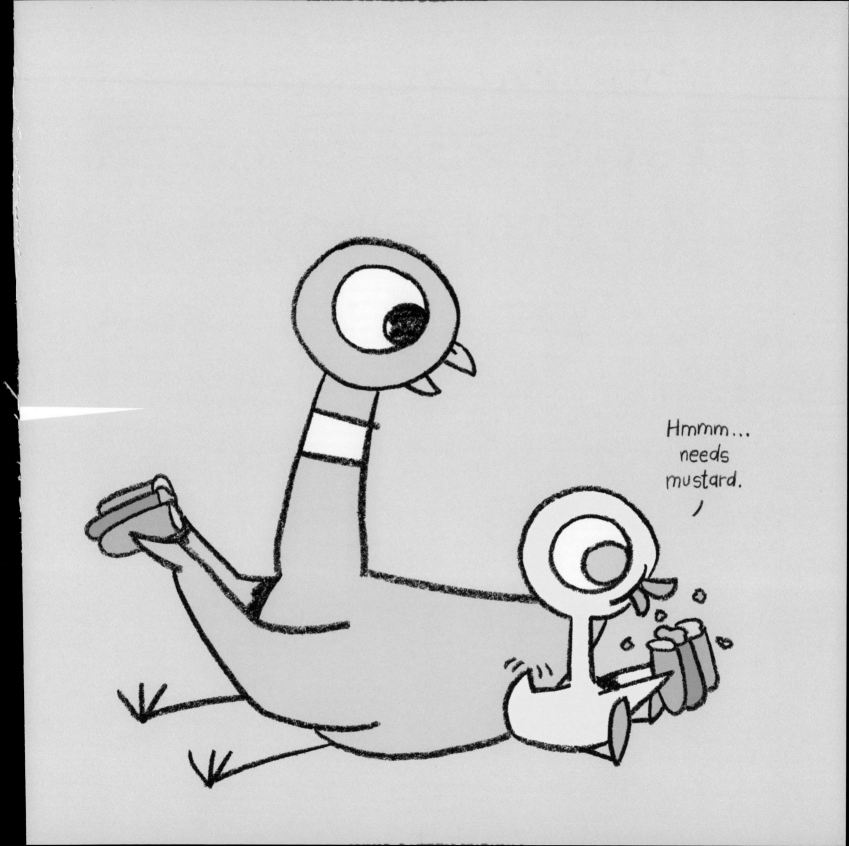